FORGEMASTERS OF THE REALM

SNÆBJÖRN

Order this book online at www.trafford.com
or email orders@trafford.com

Most Trafford titles are also available at major online book retailers.

Printed in the United States of America.

ISBN: 978-1-4669-8619-0 (sc)
ISBN: 978-1-4669-8618-3 (hc)
ISBN: 978-1-4669-8617-6 (e)

Library of Congress Control Number: 2013904876

Trafford rev. 03/14/2013

www.trafford.com

North America & international
toll-free: 1 888 232 4444 (USA & Canada)
phone: 250 383 6864 • fax: 812 355 4082

CONTENTS

Dedication

To my mother: Audrey M. Hall for teaching me the joys of reading and writing as a young man.

To Gerry Stakes, for without your guidance and love of reading, this wouldn't have been possible.

To Connie "Sissy" G. your devotion to me as I recovered from my stroke kept me going.

Map

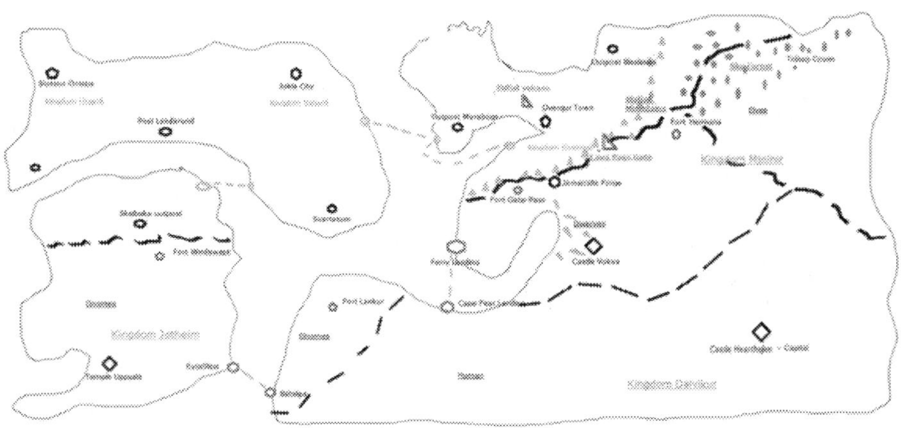

Prelude

Once upon a time as sagas commenc, strange as the world swirled around spinning tales and fables, history was constantly creating stories of heroes and antagonists. History is but a recounting of an event; it is always in the past tense, never in the present tense. History also needs an audience less history is meaningless. It matters not where the saga is recounted; the interpretations of the events of the world are in the eyes of the beholder. Thusly, this is the ancient saga of the world.

A long, long time ago, the inhabitants of the world were at peace. The races of the cosmos—be they human, dwarf, elf, gnome, goblin, orc, troll, or ogre—felt peace toward one another. All the races of the known world strived to do great things, be it creating civilizations or great arts such as paintings, writings, or education. Thusly, the great cities and empires were born out of longing to stride into the future.

The southern race of men, known as humans, eventually settled in the south and came to be known as the Kingdom of Dalvikur. The great city of the kingdom, known as Egilsstað, became a center of commerce and prosperity. In the northeast, the race of elves, which they named Kingdom Mjolnir, erected a capital called Trátop Coven. Far to the northwest, the gnomes erected Temple Uppsala, known for its wonders of invention. To the midnorth, the dwarfs constructed elaborate buildings such as the Jarnsmiða Forge, named after their trade skills.

The northern humans immigrated to the northwest, to the area known as Kingdom of Útgarð, which specialized in husbandry farming. The dwarven race settled around the Kingdom of Dvergmal and established Dvergur Stath, a center for mining. The Kingdom of Valgarð was created for the ogres, trolls, and orcs, which they named Jokla Stath, known for its hard workers. To the northwest were the race of goblins; they were an elusive lot and were known as aloof from the other races.

Then history became muddled as the races found a taste for politics. During the reign of the northen kingdom of King Ledurhaus, the world changed rapidly due to the birth of evil. The eruption of the majestic mountain Eldfjall was the cataclysmic event, cascading ash lava and death upon the northwest. Some of the listeners to the saga claimed that it was then that darkness had befallen; others said it was the birth of King Ledurhaus himself. It matters not whether the seed of destruction lay in the heart of Eldfjall or in the bosom of King Ledurhaus; the world had changed forever.

Eldfjall eruptions continued for years, unrelentingly creating havoc among the races. The north was engulfed under a cloud of spewing rocks, lava, and darkness. The torrent continued as the daylight waned from the life-giving sunlight. Within years, the north was enjoying a mini ice age, adding to the torment and agony of the inhabitants. It was as though the gods, toying with them, had turned their souls to darkness.

King Ledurhaus started to control the subjects of the kingdom, utilizing more harrowing and devious means. The guilds system was decimated; only guilds that allowed the teaching of war craft survived. The Orcs, ogres, and trolls were relegated as servants to be used only to support warriors, warlocks, and other trades involved in war. It was as if the king had linked his thirst of power to the heart of Eldfjall itself, engulfing his heart and soul to bind it with the darkness.

The effects were not exclusively confined to the northern kingdoms. As streams of refugees snaked toward the south, King Ledurhaus began to utilize his military to stem the flow of emigrants. He erected the great wall, the Lava-Gate Pass, which was constructed to deny access to the south. The military raids as well as the bandits from the north abated not, which resulted in the elves and dwarfs' seeking alliance with Egilsstað. Soon, open war engulfed the entire region.

The Great Rendering War, as the war was called, lasted for hundreds of years. It was during the initiation of the war that the advisers Svaramin and Snjofell came to be.[1] It was only a legend, but Svaramin for the north and Snjofell for the south were pawn brokers for the gods. Most of the kings and queens during the Great Rendering lived in total war, bequeathing that war to their descendants. There were great battles with victorious campaigns and losses for the combatants. The war ebbed and flowed and seemed to have no end. Thus, under the rule of King Snorri from the north and King Gjaldi from the south, the end was within grasp. King Gjaldi wielded the Great Sword Mjolnir,[2] which was forged in Jarnsmiða Forge just before the Forge fell, to slay King Snorri. The legends say that the Great Sword Mjolnir was destroyed as the result of the conflict, and Snorri perished. Others say that the Great Sword was destroyed because it was forged from the heart

---

1 Advisers offered advice to the Ruling Elites. The gods had established rules of engagement between Svaramin (evil) and Snjofell (good), which prohibited them to actively engage in battles. They could only offer counsel, a means of balance in the cosmos between good and evil.

2 The Great Sword Mjolnir was forged in Jarnsmiða, from scandium and steel, by elves with the assistance of dwarfs.

of Eldfjall, striking Snorri down. Perhaps we will never know the truth as history is in the eye of the beholder. As a result of killing Snorri, the evil curtain was born. The two sides, having killed millions of their subjects, longed for the war to cease.

With the cessation of the Great Rendering War, the world was again peaceful; though divided, the known universe had changed forever. It was through cessation of open war that, once again, civilities could progress. To this day, no prolonged war has been fought in hundreds of years; there were minor skirmishes, but no open warfare. Perhaps our ancestors, sitting around a campfire, will comment on "once upon a time . . ."

I

Going home—the sound of that was sweet music to his ears. This was his last day after five years of service to the king of the Kingdom Mjolnir.[3] Agnar was getting dressed for a party being held in his honor, a custom when soldiers leave the King's Service. Agnar was a member of Fort Hermana, under the command of Baldur. *I'll miss the men,* thought Agnar. Agnar shooed his Sekhmet, a wolverine, off his bed. Lazily his Sekhmet, named Bangsi, jumped onto the floor and curled into a ball. "Heim Til þinn," ordered Agnar, and instantly, his Sekhmet disappeared into a ball of smoke. Agnar, a ferreter by profession, had the ability to telepathically talk to his Sekhmet.[4] The command, meaning "home" or "into your cage" was always obeyed. All ferreters used Sekhmets; some used lions, others used great apes. If any foes attack a ferreter, his Sekhmet will attack immediately.

---

3 Kingdom Mjolnir: Ruled by King Runar, as part of the Realm Gustamenn.

4 Ferreter: A hunter of King's Service, with specialty in the military.

Daydreaming, he recalled his youth in Trátop Coven. Such good times were those, playing in and around the Tree of Life, dancing, playing hide-and-seek, and stealing gourd from the vines. He even recalled his first kiss: sweet Björg, beautiful creature she was. He laughed out loud at the memory of his mother when she had caught Björg and him holding hands and talking innocently about when they got older. They had not a care in the world. Suddenly, he returned to reality when Bangsi snored *weeeeeeesnortsnort* in the bed.

Agnar looked around his quarters, small, comfortable, with all the regular furnishings. As he was buttoning up his shirt, high-collared white linen with pearl buttons, he glanced in the mirror to make sure it fit right. The elf-human greeting him back was a handsome person, with almost human appearance. If not for the slightly elongated points on his ears, he looked like any normal human with golden hair. He was abnormally tall for an elf, not for a human. As he took his tabard from his bed, he heard a knock on the door. "Come."

The door opened, and in came Baldur. "Well, well, aren't you a sight for sore eyes!" exclaimed Baldur. Baldur had been his commanding officer for the last four years and looked book-perfect as a commander. He was about a head taller than Agnar. He was muscular and clean-shaven and was wearing a tabard bearing the symbol of the warrior. "I just came by to give you your severance pay and such. I shall see you at the party. The guys kinda pitched in for a good-bye present," said Baldur as he tossed a pouch onto the bed. "Oh, yes . . . You get to keep your mount as part of your wages for signing up." Baldur saluted and exited the room.

Agnar went to the bed and grabbed the pouch. Inside were five hundred Ten-Sheckles, a realm pass, and a looking glass, obviously made by the gnomes in the fort. He smiled, picked up the collapsed looking glass, and examined it. When it expanded, it allowed him to see great distances. He collapsed the looking glass and put it in the rucksack next to the bed. He was going to sorely miss his companions.

Before leaving the room, Agnar examined his surroundings. With a deep gasp of breath, he wondered if he would miss his lodgings. Before him, the sun was winking out for the evening, the pinkish-red skies falling. He stared for a bit at the garrisons' command post, the sentries lining the wall. To the right were the stables and the blacksmiths' work area. He listened to the singing of the night crickets and smelled the dung, which clung in the air. Turning to the left, he could see the serene newly lit campfires and the lances stacked against the defensive wall. The walls were made from boulders reinforced with hewn logs . . . Straight ahead was the medical facility, and beyond that was the main gate. Just beyond that lay the village. Like any defensive posts, villages always sprung up because of the soldiers. There always were the many ladies of the night, bars, and shops—like any typical shire. *Well, I guess I should get to Boars Head . . . Can't keep the people wait,* thought Agnar as he strode toward the village. He couldn't help but notice the air surrounding him: the pungent smells from the campfires, the smells from the kitchens, the occasional barking of dogs.

Entering the inn Boars Head, he was greeted with the familiar sight of mounted heads—goats, bears, lions, and deer—swords, and blunderbusses. The long tables were laden with food and drink; the smells from the table fare was scrumptious. The guests—mostly humans but some elves, dwarfs, and gnomes—gave the aroma of leathery sweat, and the perfumes from the lady guests emitted a tangy odor inside Boars Head. Gagns greeted Agnar with a "G-g-g-g-good evening, join the p-p-p-p-party" in his stammering squeaky voice. He was a tiny thing, about knee-high to Agnar, with the ability to teleport by blinking. Gagns blinked back to the bar where he was tending to the till. Agnar spotted the table with a space next to Baldur that was reserved for him, and he made his way to it. People were slapping him on the back, saying "Great to see ye," "Wish it were me," "Miss you," "Hey, short-timer," and such. Eventually, he made it to the seat and greeted Baldur. "This is a fantastic get-together. I'm honored." He could see countless people that he had worked with, including a ferreter with a tiger as his Sekhmet.

Shouting above the din, Baldur responded, "Everyone here will miss you terribly. Here, grab some briny mead." And he shoved a mug in Agnar's hand. "We have plenty of meats, breads, fruits, and most of all, women! All on us!" he exclaimed.

Agnar grinned from ear to ear as he observed that the band was coming up on the stage. With the band in full gear, the party roared its approval, laughing and showing its consent. Agnar was subscribed to dancing with one of the ladies of the night; everyone was clapping and shouting approvals. As the mead took control of the night, the partygoers were engrossed in conversations, embellished, of course, with sentry duties with Agnar. The meals were consumed zealously, calling for more meats and, of course, more mead. He was captivated with the companionship, the friendship of his companions, and the atmosphere of Boars Head.

Agnar finally made his way and sat at the table. As he took a break, he observed that Baldur was all smiles and that he truly felt a bond between them. "Let us forever keep the bond of friendship, regardless of distance or circumstances," Agnar added.

"Aye," responded Baldur, "I regard you as a brother!" Baldur saluted, brought up a mug of mead, and said, "Salute! Salute! Salute!" With that, the crowd roared, and everyone raised a mug. "Speech! Speech! Speech!" the solders cried as they banged their mugs in approval. Agnar stood and motioned for silence. "You are the most generous, pleasant, and honorable group I have ever worked with. I raise my tankard to you!" With that, the crowd went wild.

II

Homecoming was not a time of rejoicing, instead, a somber, sorrowful event. Agnar was greeted with the woeful news that his mother had died due to a scorpion sting. Because his mother was human, the sting was always fatal (elves were impervious to poisons). She was comatose within a day and died the next day. The funeral was held the day Agnar arrived; everyone was kindhearted, offering consolations and the Coven turned up in mass. The elven villagers fabricated the pyre raft, amassed the wood, and placed her gently atop. She looked regal and serene dressed in her best garb, adorned with a crown. After services were finished, the raft was set adrift, and his father, Afmyndur, set the pyre afire with a fire arrow. Agnar would not leave, even when all the members of the Coven had departed. Agnar watched the raft sink with sorrow. He was numbed by the death of his mother, dumbfounded and confused, like a lost soul that no one could console. She was a kind, gentle woman, always ready to come to his rescue when he was a lad. She will be sorely missed; her soft persuasive voice, always right when giving counsel.

"Fyrirgefa mér." Agnar was startled. Lost in thought, he didn't notice his father coming up behind him. His father, shorter than Baldur by a head, was dressed in black, as most of those people in attendance. "I am so sorry for your loss. Your mother was a wonderful person. I will always have pleasant memories of her."

"Faður minn. I don't have the words to express," choked Agnar. "If only I had departed earlier from the fort."

Afmyndur grasped both of Agnar's shoulders, stared into his eyes, and said, "Don't." His father then hugged him.

Agnar had never been hugged by his father; elves do not display public emotions. The two of them stood silent for a moment, and then Agnar hugged him back. "Come, let us go home. We need to talk," said Afmyndur.

After the two had entered the tree house, Agnar scanned the abode; the first time since he came home, really. The round door was as he remembered, with a small window in the oak wood. Memories of his mother filled his mind: meals together, when he was ill as a child, her singing in the evenings when he was sent to bed. "Do you want some melon-dew tea?" asked his father.

"Yes, please. I probably feel a bit lonely as you. What now happens in the Coven?" replied Agnar, trying to invent something to talk about.

"Ah, well, some of the Dark Elves are speaking of reconciliation.[5] But they are the exception. Here with your tea," his father said as he handed it to him. "The Coven is growing thin. Many are leaving for the south shores. Oh, lest I forget, Björg whispered to me that she wants to see you . . . She was at the service." Sipping silently on the tea, in deep contemplation, he continued, "Will you be attending the farewell event? She would like you to go. Had I died rather than your mother, I would wish you to go."

"I will go! Will Björg be attending? I have much to discuss with her."

"What are you going to do now for work? You don't need to soak in despair . . . I can help you, if you wish," offered his father. Agnar was still dressed in his traveling garb and looked forlorn about the spacious room. The table he was sitting on was on the left side of the room, a fireplace in the middle, and sitting chairs opposite to the fireplace.

"I know not, perhaps after a good night's sleep. It is good to gather my thoughts as to plans for the future," said Agnar.

The great event went well; the attendees, dressed all in black with hair wreaths, swapped memories of his mother. The mourners enjoyed typical elven food and drink. It was good to hear laughter again, strange as

---

5 Dark Elves split over the mage realm when Gjaldi crushed the alliance. Dark Elves took the majority of losses, and the Wood Elves sided with Gjaldi against King Snorri.

it sounded. There was Eyglo and his family, Erna and her daughters, and Elmar with his clan. Of course, Björg, along with her father and her brother, Dabbi, showed up. Her father, Herman, was the council lead, an important position, for the Wood Elves. As Agnar walked toward Björg, he noticed that Herman poked her on the shoulder and excused himself. "Björgmin elskan," greeted Agnar.

"I feel sorrow about your mother," said Björg. Björg was as beautiful as he had remembered before leaving to join the realm defenses. Her long black hair, adorned with flowers, flowed down toward her buttocks. She had a button nose, pink lips, and bright almond-shaped clear blue eyes. She was six years younger than Agnar, and he had been in love with her since they were children. "How do you fare?" requested Björg.

Agnar couldn't help but notice that she would not meet his eyes; she stared gloomily at the floor. "Thank you . . . I am well. I have been looking forward for years to meeting you again, but under different circumstances. How are your father and Dabbi? Are you well? What's wrong?" asked Agnar.

"Well, let us a walk. I must tell you something," she responded with a sad voice. "Dabbi must chaperone us . . . Father said that I cannot be alone with you."

After evading the guests, they finally made their way to the balcony. She continued, "Father has forbidden me to marry you. I do so love you . . . But to marry, we need to get consent from Father. I feel that as you are not of full-blooded elf, the other council members would not approve."

Dabbi interjects, "Please excuse me. I will be over by the other branch . . . Give you privacy."

Agnar placed her hands in his, gazing into her eyes. "I understand perhaps . . . But we have talked for years about marriage. I cannot live here in the Coven without you. But we cannot marry without consent"—with a half-smile attempt—"at least you are not running away with another man." He wiped a tear from her eyes.

Sobbing gently, she said, "Never, my love. I will never forget you." She pressed into his right fist a silver cameo and kissed Agnar softly. "Good-bye, my love." And she slipped away.

Stunned with the dashed dreams plus the passing of his mother, he could do nothing as he watched his love depart. His knees felt weak, falling to a kneeling position on the floor. He sat there for over an hour, pondering what next.

"My son . . . I did not have the heart to tell you. I am so sorry." Agnar heard his father's voice behind him.

"Life is such . . . It seems nothing but burdens. What will befall me now?" moaned Agnar.

"Come, my son. Perhaps you will benefit from rest. My heart aches with you. Time heals all wounds," said Afmyndur as he assisted his son to his feet. "You have suffered too much for one day. Please come and rest."

III

Sitting on his throne in Donjon Örrispa, Ormur, his head between his hands, was listening to counsel with disdain. Ormur was a demigod, offspring of the gods, not human but human in appearance. His age was unknown to mortals. He had shoulder-length black hair that obscured his face. His regal black robes were adorned with precious gems around the neck. He was holding a mace in his right hand. To his left, the entrance was staffed with two armor-clad orc sentries. The throne itself appeared to be stone, adorned with black stone gargoyles on top. Below, kneeling on the red carpet, were two Sverðingi garbed in a military dress with their helmets held in their left hands. Between them, standing on one knee, was Svaramin. Behind Svaramin was Salim-Dug, an Ápstil commander. Svaramin was dressed in a typical tan-colored warlock robe with a belt draped at his waist. "Sire, you should listen to the prophecies. Soon, the heavens will be ripe for Eldfjall to reawaken," said Svaramin. Ormur lifted his gaze on Svaramin, his cold dark eyes glistened. Ormur drank up the image before him: an old, of undetermined years, man supported by his brown ashen warlock staff.

"You are correct, Svaramin, you have always been right. We shall implement our plan immediately, and when Eldfjall wakes, we will strike a mortal blow to our enemies!" Ormur smirked as he beckoned for Haraljot. "You are responsible for increasing the outposts, especially around the Great Gate in Lava Pass. Send reinforcements, trolls, but do it quietly so as to not alert the enemy."

"As you command, Sire." Haraljot took leave from the throne room.

"And, Harasnorra, you will send more spies abroad. This is essential, gnome inventions are highly prized. You must capture as many gnomes as possible! Without the gnomes, the game will be lost. And increase by double the wyverns and wraith riders, keeping them from the border areas." Harasnorra snorted assent and, with a clinched right fist, thumped himself on the chest as a salute. "Thy will be done." And Harasnorra left the throne room.

Instructing Salim-Dug, he said, "I command you send your swiftest steeds, have your scouts reconnoiter the area near, and then the same around Temple Uppsala. *Do not* engage in combat. Report your findings to Harasnorra."

Turning back Svaramin, Ormur said, "Obtain as many ogres as you need for the new mage tower in the south. Leave me now." After Svaramin had left, Ormur let out a loud laugh in his deep voice and said, "Revenge will be mine."

Agnar fell into a deep sleep after the events of the day. Toward midnight, his mother appeared. "Sonur minn, vakna þig." *Here, Mother talking to me . . . It cannot be, is this a dream?*

She appeared in a glow, an aura that could be perceived but not touched. "I am real, my son, but not of your life. Tomorrow, you will meet Snjofell, and you must do as he instructs you. The Worm will destroy everything in its path. With long tentacles—dark, evil, multi-armed—it spares no one . . . The dark cloud descends upon us all soon. Scandium[6] must be protected and not fall in the hands of Worm." And soon, she disappeared as quickly as she appeared. Agnar woke up in a soaking sweat, the fog in his mind fighting to go free. Attempting to go back to dreamland, he found it useless. He went into the kitchen to wait for Afmyndur rising.

Afmyndur woke, dressed, and entered the kitchen for his daily melon-dew tea. He was greeted by a disheveled Agnar. "Did you have a bad sleep? You look disturbed."

"Bad dreams, I did not sleep well. Who is Snjofell?" asked Agnar.

"He is old as the ages. He always was and always will be. He attended the wedding between me and your mother. He has always been a friend of the elves, even when the Dark Elves and Wood Elves were one.

---

6 Scandium, a rare ore, which Thor gave to the dwarfs, was used for re-forging the great sword.

I know not if he is human. Never asked him. You don't remember him. You were four years of age when he came to visit last. Why do you ask?"

"I know not why I asked. Must have had a dream, I suppose," replied Agnar. "Tell me about the elven clans. What happened to split the clans?"

With a wistful look in his eyes, Afmyndur replied, "It was during the reign of Gjaldi when King Snorri was slain with the Great Sword. Apparently, the Great Sword shattered during the battle. Well, after the clash, Gjaldi was a changed man. He had taken counsel, and laws were enacted that were detrimental to the elves. The elves were shown disrespect and not invited to council meetings. To make a short story, the Dark Elves left the alliance eventually. The Wood Elves stayed with the alliance."

"And what happened to the sword?" asked Agnar. "Where did the sword come from?"

"The sagas state that the sword was forged by a Dark Elf[7] with the help of a dwarf. Allegedly, the ore used was provided by Thor himself, but no one knows if it is true. The elves gave the Great Sword to Gjaldi as a symbol to bolster his campaign against Snorri, as a gift from the gods." As Afmyndur paused a minute, he then continued, "I don't know where the sword is now. At any rate, it is useless as it is just shards and a hilt."

---

7 Dark elves were artistically inclined and forged a unique sword with an amber stone hilt. The dwarf was a master at the forge, smelting the ores used for the Great Sword.

Agnar was startled by the knock on the door. He excused himself, opened the door, and found himself face-to-face with an older gentleman. He was dressed in all white, in a mage's robe, and supported himself with a white cane. The cane was about the same length as Snjofell was tall, with a translucent globe on the top of the cane, fixed with wooden fingers wrapped around the globe. With his intelligent blue eyes, long flowing gray beard, and shoulder-length white hair, he knew immediately that it was Snjofell. He was stunned. *So it was true,* thought Agnar.

"Well, should I enter or stand out?" queried Snjofell.

"I am so sorry . . . Please come in . . . come in. May I offer you some melon-dew tea?" Agnar apologized profusely.

When Afmyndur rose to greet his guest, he smiled and hailed, "Snjofell, my old friend. Come in, please do come in." And he gestured to a chair at the table. "Sorry Sif could not greet you. She had an accident with a scorpion and is no longer with us."

"Yes, please accept my condolences. I came as fast as I could after I heard the news. Agnar, you have grown up since the last I saw you," Snjofell said. "We have much to talk about." Snjofell stared at Agnar. "And I spoke to your mother last night, and I suspect you had conversation last night also."

IV

<u>Spies among us</u>*, the abundance of intelligence indicates that something is going to happen soon.* Gagns had reported that strangers were coming in the Boars Head and asking strange questions about gnomes. There had been an increase in rumors asking for names of gnomes living in the outer areas in farms, working with heitapipur. Baldur changed his train of thought, and Baldur found himself in awe of the Castle Hearthglen. The building, which contained the throne, was massive with a huge statue of Gjaldi resting on his broadsword. The building was draped with long woven silk banners throughout.

The inhabitants, mostly humans, were buzzing about with the daily tasks of living. Everywhere were the smells of commerce: from the shops, taverns, and inns. Everyone was smiling, obviously out of contentment. The capital city had been laid out into districts, the trade quarter, the industrial district, the banking square, and the mage area. The Realm Bank and Guild Banks offered services for the flow of commerce. The city was obviously well guarded, with sentries posted throughout the citadel, and the Megalopolitan was surrounded with a moat. The main gate did not utilize a drawbridge but rather a paved roadway into the city. Everywhere were gardens with myriad-colored flowers. Almost every building within the citadel sported magnificent works of arts.

Baldur fell thinking upon the gnomes—such a different race of people; not of dwarfs, not of elves, but a mixture of both dwarfs and elves. They were similar to leprechauns in that they shared ideas about religions and financial matters, and they were also similar in stature and size. But leprechauns have not been seen for centuries, if they existed at all. The gnomish realm, also known as the Kingdom Jotheim, was a different race of people—different from the other realms of the kingdom. Kingdom Jotheim, under the leadership of Smakongur, they were well educated, multilingual, and generally well-to-do. Spending efforts to create a diverse culture, they were one that were not interested in military matters and security. But why should they since security and military matters were left to the other kingdoms? It showed with all the diverse cultural buildings, educational systems, and political dislike of change. On the surface, it was full of museums, theaters, educational vocations of the inhabitants, minarets, open markets, different types of music in the loft. It appeared, like a wonderful realm; underneath, though, it was a different story.

Over the decades, as the gnomish people grew aloof from their leadership, it was easy picking for the bureaucrats, allowing the ruling class to create dynasties. The laypeople gnomes were ruled by one set of laws while the bureaucrats lived under another set of laws. Corruption was widespread, with little or nothing done to stem it. Thusly, with little or no military influence, while the other kingdoms foot the bill with no requirement of their own assets, the northern borders were rife with intruders from the north. Trading between bands of enterprise gangs and gnomish people went almost unchecked. It was commonplace to see ogre and orcs wandering over the border and, occasionally, bands of Árapstil people from the north.

But by the time the few and far-distant fort patrols came, the interlopers were gone. Of course, the gnomish leadership blamed the small intrusions with the killings and thefts in their kingdom upon the forts; it was easier to accuse the forts of the lack security, and of course, the politicians took advantage wherever they could. After all, the forts were manned by men (mostly), and gnomes weren't of men; they were gnomes, easier to blame men.

The Kingdom Jotheim languished from the same centuries-old problem of other kingdoms: low interest of responsibility on the personal citizenry of its peoples. In other words, they became used to not having to be bothered with civic duties and left it to their politicians. Baldur was intoned to believe that the gnome realm was rife with spies and confederates with other races.

He was waiting to be called before Queen Audri, and he wanted to persuade her about his concerns. Suddenly, one of her counselors shouted ENTER to Baldur. After entering the throne anteroom and bowing to the queen, Baldur started, "Your Highness, I bring you news of an increase of spies from the north."

Queen Audri, flanked to her left with a counselor, appeared to be a late-aged woman with cold glassy eyes and long red hair topped by a tiara. Her regal robes did her alluring figure justice, and her long blue-painted fingernails caught the visitor's eye. Her counselor, named Ormskepna, whispered into her ear and then stated, "I am aware of your suspicions. I am also aware that you are displeased that we have cut your troop's size. How much of this "new intelligence" is valid, or are you decrying your position on our realm defenses?"

Baldur was repulsed by Ormskepna, with greasy shoulder-length black hair and a thin face with a long nose. "Yes, Your Highness, I have complied with your wishes about the defenses, but I can assure you that I am not blowing hot air about the intelligence," stated Baldur.

"Silence. You dare question my decisions? I have the resources of the realm at my disposal, and you are only a troop commander," retorted the queen; her ashen face showed no emotions. The counselor whispered again into her ear and, after a short pause, added, "But I will take your observations under consideration. Perhaps I will form a team to study the matter. You may now leave, I have other important duties to attend to. You may attend the palace ball this evening, if you wish."

Baldur bowed and stated, "As you wish, My Highness." *A team to study the matter . . . They would be months or years before that ever happens,* thought Baldur as he left the throne room. Turning toward the counsel waiting in the hall, he asked, "I think I will attend the ball. What time does it start?"

"After sundown, shall I send an escort for you?" replied the counselor.

"Yes, please, that would be fine." Baldur smiled. *Yes, though I'd be doing of some intelligence gathering tonight myself,* thought Baldur.

Baldur had finished getting dressed for the royal ball when a knock came on the door. Donning his tabard, he opened the door and was met by a gorgeous young lady dressed to the hilt. "Wow, you look beautiful this evening."

"Thank you. I am Zonda from the council public affairs staff. I trust you will not bore me to death with politics tonight," said Zonda.

"I bet you already know all about me—I am no politician. I plan on enjoying myself this evening, with such a lovely woman on my arm," Baldur smiled as he spoke. Zonda blushed slightly and offered her arm. "Anyone important to be attending this evening that would be interested in me?"

"Why would you say that? I don't keep tabs on all the guests," replied Zonda.

"Oh, just wondering why you were chosen to be my escort for the evening. And I'm sure that the council will want to be debriefed tomorrow." Baldur smiled as he continued, "But I will be on my best honor, so nothing to report!"

Upon nearing the ballroom, a page was announcing the guests. When the couple was next, two trumpeters blew three blasts, and the page shouted, "Announcing Commander Baldur Arnarsson and Lady Zonda Loftsdottir!" They were escorted into the royal ballroom, which was a massive place, lavishly decorated with tables stacked with food and drinks. A band was playing, soft music wafting throughout the ballroom. There were about two hundred guests, representative of all the races in the southern realms. Zonda was a stunning sight; she knew all the right protocols and fit perfectively with the crowd, almost as if she were royalty herself. The evening was perfect.

Svaramin was surveying the area around the construction of the Svartaturn, the new black tower. He was pleased so far. To his right were the camps housing Dobamen and his cavalry Ápstil. The pit was dug into the ground and was built up for the replication of the orcs, with hovels dug into the walls of the pit. He could see the ogres and trolls pulling massive stone slabs for the construction of the Svaraturn. The pit was swarming with slaves chained together: the dwarfs mining the ores and others working as stone cutters, the lesser orcs doing manual labor, and the gnomes that were used as architects and were working on the heitapipur. He was content with the progress so far, with new slave trains coming every other day with slaves from the south. His stable used for the flugapets was suitable, where he could house his wyvern. He needed to report back on the progress and ask for more supplies, stolen from the south, of course. He mounted his wyvern and flew off to the northwest.

Snjofell recounted the message that Sif had given to him and Agnar. Afmyndur was dumbfelt, unable to grasp the events of the dream. "We have much to do and very little time to do it. When the onslaught begins, we need to have an evacuation plan ready. Perhaps, Afmyndur, you should lead your people to a place of safety, what about Fort Hermana? Do you think you can convince any of the Dark Elves with allegiance to evacuate too?"

"No, my people will not rely on the humans. I would have more success with the Dark Elves if we rely on the elven clans, maybe get to safety to the southern part of the realm. We have little use for humans, they have proven over and over that they are greedy and power-hungry," averred Afmyndur.

"Snjofell, what are we going to do? Do you have a plan? I know that Fort Hermana has cut its defenses not long ago, and the villages and farms need a place of safety to go. I agree with Afmyndur, though. Don't count on the humans," Agnar gazed upon Snjofell as he replied.

"Very well, contact the Dark Elves and convince as many as will be willing to move at the right time. Also, it is important that Bogamaður[8] be willing to relinquish the Great Sword hilt. It must be returned back to the elven clans. As for us, Agnar and I will alert Fort Hermana before we go to visit the dwarfs in Castle Vokva. I still have good relations with the dwarfs, so I should be able to enlist their help," explained Snjofell.

Afmyndur interjected, "That will be tough, trying to get them to believe that we want to help. No one knows where the Great Sword is, just the hilt. And why give up the hilt? It is useless without the sword, and unless you have a plan to re-forge the Great Sword, it would of no use."

"I have a plan, my old friend, but we need scandium," replied Snjofell.

Arriving at Fort Hermana, the party asked who was in charge. The sentries at the main gate, recognizing Agnar, saluted. "Baldur is in Castle Hearthglen on business. The second in command is in the command

---

8 Bogamaður is the leader of the Dark Elves' rebels.

post," stated the sentry as he opened the gate. After reaching the command post, they were challenged by the guards at the door. "I have business with the commander. It is imperative that I speak to him at once! Do you recognize Agnar?" Snjofell commanded as he pointed toward Agnar.

"At once, I will escort you to him," acknowledged the guard.

After formally exchanging greetings with Lt. Foringi, they stated that the fort needed to get ready for refugees from the dark times to come. "Yes, we have been infiltrated within the last few days. There were reports of spies and people asking strange questions. Baldur should be back tomorrow. But I cannot increase patrols, we don't have enough troops," replied Lieutenant Foringi.

"At least you need to make provisions for the safety of the inhabitants in the area around the fort. I behoove you to heed my warnings," expounded Snjofell. "I know that raiding parties have increased to the west around Castle Vokva and further and beyond. Many farms have been destroyed, and some slave trains have been spotted moving to the north."

"Good idea. I can put an alarm bell up on the perimeter wall to warn the villagers to come here for safety," said Foringi.

Agnar thanked Foringi and suggested that they drop by the Boars Head Inn to get some supplies and that they could question some of the villagers and have them spread the word about the warning bell.

Gagns was excited when they entered the inn. "D-d-d-d-d-did you h-h-h-hear about the spies? I t-t-told Baldur about them. Can I g-g-g-g-get you s-s-something to eat, maybe a r-r-r-room?"

Agnar, pointing toward Snjofell, said, "Gagns, this is Snjofell. Yea, we will be glad to dine here and take a room for the night. Oh, we will need some supplies before we head off to Castle Vokva." Agnar smiled. "When you are not busy, can you drop by and talk a bit? I have a lot of questions for you about the strangers that have been around."

Gagns confirmed the order then blinked toward the kitchen area. In a few minutes, he returned with the meal and accepted a seat at the table. "What do y-y-y-you want to k-k-k-know?"

After sipping some mead, Snjofell started the questioning. "Can you describe the strangers? Do you know how many of them were here? What type of answers were they after?"

"Hmmmm . . . Let me see . . . They w-w-w-w-were dressed in hooded cloaks, w-w-w-we never could see their f-f-f-faces. I think t-t-they were humanoids. We only s-s-saw two of them, riding h-h-h-huge black horses. They d-d-didn't say exactly what t-t-they wanted, just t-t-t-they were asking about gnomes," responded Gagns. His face twisted into a fearful feature. "M-m-m-maybe I need to c-c-c-check on my brother. H-h-he owns a Konglo farm to t-t-the west of town."

"Maybe we can escort you to your brother's farm, we are heading west anyway. We would be pleased to ride with you tomorrow," interjected Agnar.

"Hmmm, huge black horses . . . humanoids . . . I suspect they are Ápstil. I would have to see them in person to be sure," stated Snjofell. "I have had many encounters with them over the years."

"You are very k-k-k-kind. I will be glad to r-r-r-ride with you in the m-m-morning. Shall I wake y-y-you in the morn?" said Gagns with a smile on his face.

The trio was saddled up and ready to go. They were a strange group, Agnar on Closu, Snjofell sitting on his snow-white mare, and Gagns posing on a miniature pony. The cold bite this morning was evidence that winter was preparing to envelope the world. The starlit skies, with its quarter moon, made the journey easier. "It won't be long before sunset. Tell me about your brother," asked Snjofell.

"You m-m-mean Biggy? He was a h-h-hunter like Agnar, stationed here for many years. He finished h-h-his service, bought some l-l-land, and started a Konglo farm," replied Gagns. "He doesn't c-c-come to visit often, he i-i-i-is a loner."

"Ah, so he is a hunter. Does he use a bow or a sword?" questioned Snjofell.

"He was an advanced s-s-swordsman. Best one of the best too." Gagns smiled. It was obvious that he admired Biggy.

Soon, as the sun crept over the horizon, they were almost there. Suddenly, Agnar bolted up in his saddle and cried, "Ápstil, two of them, one of them battling a Konglo, the other throwing a net! Bangsi, Komdu!" And his Sekhmet obeyed instantly. Gagns was already galloping at a breakneck speed toward Biggys horse with Snjofell not far behind. "Seize 'em," he commanded Bangsi. The Konglo was spitting web upon one of them, gluing him to the ground. Soon he would be wrapped in a cocoon, ready for the paralyzing stings. Agnar readied his bow, speeding ahead on Closu, targeting the other Ápstil. *Phew!* It sounded as the arrow sang toward its destination. Bangsi leaped back just as the arrow sank deep into his back. The aggressor died almost immediately. Gagns, having reached his brother, tore a knife into the netting.

"What took you guys so long?" complained Biggy.

Biggy was disheveled after the ordeal and busied himself by brushing off the dirt. He was a little taller than Gagns, and sported a gray beard; he was adorned in a brown vest over a white shirt and green pants. His Sekhmet was safeguarding Biggy, wary of the strangers around him. The Konglo was of the giant species, black, with a red tuft of hair on his head. His jaws were massive, and his two front legs being longer than the back ones. Bangsi was circling the Konglo, sniffing the legs in order to ascertain what manner of beast it was.

Snjofell went to examine the Ápstil, which was still encased in the cocoon. Agnar turned over the dead Ápstil, scanning the face of the intruder. "So what happened here?" challenged Agnar. "Why were they after you?" Looking at Biggy, waiting for an answer, he was busy stroking his Konglo to calm the Sekhmet.

"Who is this?" asked Biggy as he turned toward Gagns.

"Agnar, hunter by profession, from the Woods Elves clan." He extended a hand toward Biggy and disarmed him with a smile.

"Well, I had heard that some strangers were asking questions of gnomes, so I lied to them. Told 'em that I was working in the Gufaheita. Then they attacked me," replied Biggy. "I could have took 'em. My Sekhmet, Attafot protected me."

"I didn't s-s-see you taking them on! As f-f-far as I could s-s-s-see, you were under a net," offered Gagns contrarily.

Looking around for the steeds, Agnar noticed that the farm was dug into a hill and beyond that was a cave entrance. This must be where the Konglo were sheltered. The abode that Biggy was living in was about five feet tall. "Let's discuss about it later, I'll load up the two Ápstils, we should take them to the fort. Maybe you should come with us. We don't want them to return if they had reinforcements."

To that, Biggy said, "I'll just gather some things then, I won't be long." Biggy and Gagns entered the home while the steeds were corralled by Agnar.

Both Snjofell and Agnar loaded up the two steeds, strapping the bodies down.

"Snjofell," said Agnar, "this is enough evidence for the kingdom to act. If only we could get the other kingdoms to unite."

Shortly, the two gnomes exited from the house, with Biggy clad in mail armor and bearing his sword. He bore his rucksack, filled with useful things found in the home, and he blinked and found himself astride Gagns' pony. Biggy dismissed his Sekhmet and added, "I hope my Konglo herd will be safe."

Fort Hermana was just over the hill. They spotted a patrol from the fort coming toward them, flying to the fort banner. Leading the patrol was Baldur. Shortly, as they neared the group, Baldur hailed, "'Lo . . . What news? What are you doing there, Biggy? Are you coming back to join up again with the kingdom?" He pointed to the two steeds bearing the bound bodies. "I see that you have two Ápstil, one looks to be alive. We should interrogate him. Follow us back to the fort."

"Nay, Baldur, I come not to join again. I was captured, but my companions saved me." Biggy laughed in the direction of Baldur and added, "Aye, let *me* interrogate them. I'll make him talk."

Agnar interrupted, "Now we have evidence such to prove to Queen Audri that we need more troops here at the fort." After a short pause, he added, "I fear for the kingdom, but I have some bad news. The elves will not assist the humans. I warned them, but the elves will have no part in defending the kingdom. Already, many of them are flowing to the south as refugees to avoid the violence to come."

"We are heading west, towards Citadel Vokva, to warn them and to see if we can enlist some help," said Snjofell. "You should send a messenger to Queen Audri as soon as possible."

"I have just come back from the capitol, attended a hearing at the queen's court. I am not certain that she will respond," Baldur replied sadly. "I think I have an ally within the castle, I shall send a message as soon as I can."

Biggy piped in, "Aye, then I will go with you. I know many dwarfs, and I can recruit some troops. Besides, the North Alliances have targeted us gnomes—I want revenge!"

V

Citadel Vokva was a huge sprawling castle, hewed entirely of stone. The citadel's main gate was only accessed via a huge drawbridge; under it was a moat, making it almost impregnable. Atop the gate was a massive archway with a stone statue of a dwarf, standing vigilantly with a hammer held high over his head. Just beyond the gates, the cobblestone roads were littered with merchants and with shops, inns, and guild offices. On display outside of the shops were armored suits, various ores, and gems crafted by the dwarfs. The throng of inhabitants—mostly dwarfs, some gnomes, few elves, and a handful of humans—were scurrying here and there, doing business. The air was alive with smells from the inns, the soft waft of music, and the laughter from the children playing in the streets.

"Well, here we are. Now to greet the citadel rulers of the city," said Snjofell gleefully.

Baldur had finished with the interrogation of the captured spy. He learned that the Lava Pass had been reinforced, but he didn't know why or how many troops. He did know that the wyvern and wraith riders had been increased and that the Northern Alliance was looking for slaves, particularly gnomes and dwarfs. Little more was gleaned from him, so Baldur ordered the execution of the spy. This was dire news, so he decided to pen a missive to Zonda as he did not trust the queen. Taking a quill pen to paper, Baldur wrote,

"My Lady Zonda, Egilsstað:

I write you to warn you of instances, which have dire consequences for the kingdom. Unfortunately, I have no one to turn to except for you; I have to trust you since I have allegiance with the Castle Egilsstað. I do not trust the confidential counsel that the Queen Audi is receiving. I have captured a spy from the Northern Alliance, which confirms that we are on the verge of open war. I trust that you will do the right thing, warn the queen, and initiate subscription for all able-bodied people in the kingdom. I feel that you will assist us in repelling any invaders. Please take good care that this missive does not fall into the hands of untrustworthy subjects; trust no one. Spies are all around within the castle.

Faithfully,
Baldur"

After sealing the message with the seal of the fort, Baldur dispatched a soldier on the fastest steed in the stable. "Make sure *nobody* except for Lady Zonda, not even the queen herself, will read this! That is an order, protect it with your life." And he watched the rider gallop off. Baldur then turned to Lieutenant Foringi and ordered that the garrisoned troops be on full alert until further notice.

Baldur went to Boars Head to talk to Gagns. He found him busily washing up the pots and pans in the kitchen. "'Allo, do you have a minute?" Gagns smiled and nodded pointing to a chair in the kitchen.

After cleaning the utensils, Gagns said, "That's d-d-done. What d-d-do you need?"

"Well, I was wondering if your brother has any silk out at the farm. One of the dwarfs in the village can make extra body armor for the troops. I know that the dwarfs can fashion extra strong armor using the silk." Baldur paused a few seconds then said, "I wanted to know if you can control the Konglos at the farm. They are as good as troop reinforcements in case if the fort comes under attack."

"Hmmm . . . I used to h-h-help out on the farm. I d-d-don't know if I can control t-t-them or not, though," responded Gagns. "I can r-r-round up several b-b-bolts of silk, though. Biggy m-maybe will not like it, no aura. He will g-g-g-get over it, though."

Grinning at Gagns, Baldur said, "I will pay you for the bolts. I'll dispatch an escort for you. Get as much as you can find. If the Konglos will obey you, maybe we should corral them at the fort. If we come under attack, we should arm the citizenry in the defense of the fort."

Svaramin accomplished about three-fourths of his Svartaturn, looking pleased over the landscape. He was accompanied by Harasnorra, discussing the construction project. Surveying the upcoming weather clouds, he said, "Winter is coming soon. We need to double the production before we are snowed in. Looks like maybe some snow later on today. We lost some of our spies because of enemy action. Why don't you concentrate on capturing more gnomes and dwarfs? Cut back on the spies. With the onslaught of winter, there isn't much more that we can do. I want this tower finished within a fortnight."[9] Svaramin pointed toward the pit and beckoned Harasnorra. "We need to erect the heitapipur down in the pit so our Orcs have some heat for the winter. We also need to use the pipes to commence with the forges. We need armor and weapons for our Orcs."

"I will have the gnomes start on them right away," replied Harasnorra.

"I will leave you so you can start working on your tasks," commented Svaramin. He then entered the tower, climbed three floor steps, and entered the door to his right. *I should scry,*[10] *don't want to get caught off guard,* thought Svaramin. He placed his crystal ball

9 Fortnight: Two weeks long

10 *Scry*, or *scrying*, is the use of a clear magic ball that allows warlocks to read future events or to locate objects.

on the table and commenced to scry. Svaramin, with a twisted grin on his face, said, "Snjofell, my old friend, we shall once again meet in combat! Hmm . . . What are you doing in Vokva?" Suddenly, Svaramin, sensing that Snjofell was looking directly at him, covered his crystal ball and aborted his scrying.

Magnus embraced Snjofell with glee. "Long time we have not met. Welcome, my old friend." Magnus was a typical dwarf: barrel-chested with huge arms and broad shoulders. His red hair and beard were a henna-red color and braided. The Hall of Heroes was adorned with life-sized marble statues depicting the dwarven heroes. "And who do we have here? Are you not a human?" he asked, talking to Agnar and extending a hand as greeting. He smiled.

Agnar bent down to bow and accept the warm greeting, saying, "Sire, I am Agnar of the Woods Elves clans—half human. And this is Biggy from the Farm Bleusgrof, outside of Fort Hermana."

"Welcome, my new friends. Come share a table with me while we talk of old times," directed Magnus toward Snjofell. Turning toward his valet, he clapped his hands and ordered a meal for his guests. He asked Agnar, "Have you ever been to Vokva before?"

"Nay, Your Highness, I have always wanted to come to visit," responded Agnar. "But we have come here under much distress. But we should discuss this matter later."

Biggy interjected in a squeaky voice, "Is the Two-Fishes Inn still open? I hope to meet some gnomes that I know there."

"Aye, it is, my friend. Feel free to browse through the city," Magnus answered as he smiled at Biggy.

After the meal, the king and his guests enjoyed a smoke, the vapors swirling about from the pipes. "So, Snjofell, what brings you here? Surely you are not here as a friendly visit," asked Magnus. "Agnar hinted about your quest, and yeah, I know of some rumors and intelligence matters."

Wincing, Snjofell agreed, saying, "Aye, these are dark times ahead." He recounted the events preceding the visit. "I beseech you for some assistance. Queen Audri has not taken good care of the kingdom, and with little help for the other kingdoms of the realm. Particularly, there have been increased raids from the North Alliances, taking captives of gnomes and dwarfs."

With a pained look on his face, Magnus answered, "Aye, there has been ever increasing incursions, and it pains me to say yes, dwarfs have been captured. Some of the outlaying farms have been attacked, but it seems they were looking for plunder, not necessarily just slaves."

Agnar interjected, "Tell us about the Forge. Why was it abandoned? I assume that it was built by dwarfs."

"Aye, it was built under the rule of King Hauster. It was a thriving capital city of the dwarfs, with mining, jewel makers, weapon and armor smiths. The location was perfect as Mount Eldfjall was tapped for the lava flows, which, in turn, fueled the Great Forge. Scandium can only be produced with lava as it is the only thing hot enough to forge with. After King Snorri was slain, and the Great Sword was destroyed, Eldfjall went dormant. Violent earthquakes plagued Jarnsmiða. Great fissures were created because of them, which resulted in the abandonment of the city," explained Magnus.

Pausing for a few seconds, Snjofell added, "I have a plan for reuniting the elves' clans, and they will be willing to shore up the defenses. But . . ." After a pregnant pause, he continued, "I need the shards of the Great Sword and some scandium—I intend to re-forge the sword!"

"By the gods," thundered Magnus. "How do you to intend to do that? We don't have the hilt, and even if we had it, that would mean having to travel to Jarnsmiða forge—restart it. The forge hasn't been used for centuries, and the heitapipur have been blocked. No one has entered the Jarnsmiða since those days, and no living creature dares trespass. Not even the forces in the Northern Alliances."

"I know the obstacles before us are formidable, but these are dire times. We can find gnomes that have heitapipur knowledge, and we can enlist a volunteer dwarf to man the forge," suggested Snjofell. "We must do this, we have no choice."

Biggy piped up, "I know a gnome here in Vokva that I think we can get him to volunteer."

"Well, the matter is settled," said Magnus. "Why don't you and Agnar and Biggy see what you can do? Snjofell, follow me into the vaults then and get the shards. Then we shall see about getting the scandium then."

The Two-Fishes tavern was in the center of Castle Vokva, flanked by a hanging advertisement of two fishes with crossed tails. The laughter and smell of ales hung in the air. Biggy and Agnar entered through the double doors, when suddenly, Biggy was assaulted by a chubby-faced female gnome, who grabbed him by the ear and slapped his head.

"You dog! You miserable cur! How dare you show your face in here?" she wailed at Biggy, cursing.

"But . . . but . . . darling, I . . ." Biggy apologized profusely as he tried to avoid her grasp.

"Don't you 'darling' me! Where have you been? I want some answers and not some mamby-honey stuff from you," demanded his attacker. "I was engaged to you, and then you disappear without a trace and no explanation."

"Ahh, lover's quarrel. That explains." Agnar laughed. The female gnome was gruff in appearance, dressed in trousers and a brown shirt, with short golden hair styled as two buns upon her head.

"I . . . I was going to send for you, I promise . . . Why, I even bought a farm for us to live in outside of Fort Hermana," stammered Biggy.

She squinted with one eye, apparently to make up her mind if he was telling the truth. She eventually let go of the ear, swollen and red. "What kind of fool to you think I am?" she asked, not sure if she wanted to believe him. "I even kept your ring, but then sold it. Why would I want to take up with you again?"

"M-m-my love, my dearest love—," started Biggy.

"You can't fool me again! A farm . . . What kind of farm? Are you lying to me again?" asked his ex-fiancée. "And WHAT are you doing going around with a HUMAN?"

"He 'tisn't a human, he is my journey companion. Agnar is his name, from the Woods Elves clan." Biggy was rubbing his ear to make sure it was intact. "Ask him, he can tell you that I have a Konglo farm."

"Well, obviously, you two know each other . . . Yes, I am Agnar; I am at your service." And he bowed graciously. "And yes, he does indeed own the farm. And may I call you . . ." He waited for a response from the female gnome.

She paused, squinted, and said, "SiSi be my name, and I don't know if I want to talk with you . . . You have poor choices for friends."

Agnar smiled at her and said, "While you meet many people in this life, when journeys take you hither and thar, you sometimes meet people you don't intend to extend a hand of friendship." Biggy stuck out his tongue at Agnar, not knowing what he had just said. "Please accept my invitation to our table."

SiSi blushed a little bit, and having been disarmed by his grace, she accepted. "And no funny business, and I be not ready to allow you to worm your way in on me either," she responded directly to Biggy.

After drinking several ales, Agnar and Biggy recounted the tales of the journey. Obviously, SiSi still felt warm toward Biggy despite the greeting they had received. "I will join your group. I not be fooled again." SiSi stared directly at Biggy. "I can be of much use to the group. Usable because of my mage training. I want to keep an eye on you."

Snjofell followed Magnus into the vaults. Inside were plunder from various campaigns, works of arts, and national treasures. Coming across a locked glass case just to the right of the vault, Snjofell saw what he was looking for. Lying on a bed of purple velvet were five shards and a scabbard. "Ah, there it is . . . I'll open the case, and then you can take it," murmured Magnus. "Now for the scandium . . . Let me see where it be . . . Ah, yes, yes . . . over here." Magnus picked up an iron box, closed it, and said, "I don't want to be around when you open the box. Scandium does evil things to those who touch it."

Snjofell gave a black cloth to Magnus to cover the box. "I have no intention to touch it . . . I was there when it was used to smite Snorri," added Snjofell. "Now to find a dwarf that can use the forge."

"Aye, I know the perfect candidate. A paladin by trade, but good smithy too, and being a paladin, he will be perfect for our needs. He can heal as well as wield a sword and a blunderbuss. The quest we are on is extremely dangerous. Perhaps we should swear him to secrecy," said Magnus. "I'll summon him in the morrow, he needs to stock up at the alchemists, get some mage bandages."[11]

Early in the morning, the group roused just before dawn. The quarters they had been given was splendid, luxuriously furnished, and had a fireplace. Soon after, SiSi dropped in as she dusted off the snow from the short walk between their quarters and her home. "*Brr,* cold this morn." She shivered slightly and walked toward the fireplace to warm up. After the greetings were exchanged, the troop walked to the Hall of Heroes where Magnus was already present. In front of him was an unusually tall dwarf on one knee. He was clad in shiny heavy armor, which bore upraised color and adorned with socketed Gemshard Heart gems.[12] Next to the paladin was his valet, a gnome by race.

"Good day, I trust you had a pleasant night," greeted Magnus to the troop. My paladin here,

---

11 Mage bandages are used for healing by paladins. They are made from mage cloth.

12 Precious gems are often used by warriors, paladins, and hunters to bolster attributes of their armor. Gemshard Heart is one of the many gems used. Depending on the gem, it does offer different attributes to the armor.

Dabbilus by name, and his valet, Smari.[13] They have agreed to accompany your company, and they have been sworn to an oath." Dabbilus sported a stomach-long red braided beard and metal wristbands, and was carrying a broadsword.

"Sire, you can call me Dabs," stated Dabbilus to Snjofell. "And this is my trusted valet, Smari, a gnome trained in heitapipur."

"Please dispense of the formalities, I am Snjofell," replied Snjofell, and he began to introduce the group.

For several days, the troop lounged around the castle, waiting for the snow to stop. It was good, though, because they discussed plans for the upcoming trek. They had agreed that once the sword was reforged, they would light the bonfires located in the old abandoned outposts. Magnus would send a small band of troops to man the six bonfires. Snjofell and Agnar would go try to have the Dark Elves sit in counsel and attempt to attach the hilt once the sword was made whole again. The plan is that if the signal lights up, then the Dark Elves would join in the defense of the realm, if the Dark Elves agree—a big IF. The four other members would trek up the mountain and try to get access to Jarnsmiða Forge.

---

13 All soldiers of the classes of warrior and paladin have a valet, a person who is under training and helps the soldier with armor, weapons, and mounts.

VI

Zonda finished reading the missive. With remorse, she penned a response.

"Commander Baldur, Fort Hermana:

I received your missive. I cannot concede to your request. I have no influence over Queen Audi as her counselor Ormskepna blocks access to the queen. You are correct about the spies in the citadel. If you can, I will meet you at a farm named Joldugrof, just north of Egilsstað, in five days. I have destroyed your missive to me.

Lady Zonda, Egilsstað"

She sealed the message, placed a royal seal on it, and commanded a lady-in-waiting to deliver it to Commander Baldur at Fort Hermana. She had the lady-in-waiting to swear an oath, which only Baldur should read it, upon pain of death if she fails to deliver it.

Snjofell and Agnar had saddled their mounts after Snjofell had relinquished the iron box and the shards to Dabs. He instructed him to not open the box; if he did, Svaramin would immediately sense the scandium, resulting in the North Alliance to commence an attack on them. "We shall return on the third day. We will meet you at the Jarnsmiða Forge entrance," instructed Snjofell. It was still snowing but was lessening. The cobblestone streets glistened in the daylight, and he added, "Do not enter the forge itself, wait for us to return. We will ride as fast as possible. If it stops snowing, commence the journey, lest start out tomorrow."

Salim-Dug sat on his steed with his cape, trying to ward the cold winds away from him. The snorting coming from his mount was dispelling massive clouds from his nostrils, as the front paws were shoveling at the tundra. Ahead lay Fort Windswept, barely visible from this distance. He had established a listening post overlooking the road leading the fort. The fort had approximately 250 troops stationed there, but at any given time, there were only about seventy-five on duty, with change of the guards approximately nine hours apart.

The small village just outside of the fort was of no concern. The walls around the fort were made of wooden stakes, sharpened on the tips, and boulders. A small moat had been dug around the perimeter. They appeared to be well armed and sent patrols out about every seven hours apart. Kingdom Jotheim seemed to be lightly defended, given the size of the kingdom. He estimated that any reinforcements from Temple Uppsala would need at least nine hours to reach the fort at a fast pace.

The gnomes seemed to rely too much on the humans from Castle Hearthglen, as most of the defenders were indeed human. The countryside in Jotheim seemed to be a scrub tundra, with bogs and little forested areas and hills. Troop movements would be very tedious with the onset of winter. The goblins in the demilitarized zone[14] would have less problems with the winters, though. The outpost Skelbaka could be easily reinforced from the north, making resupplying of their troops much better—that, and the ferry, would be able to constantly ship troops. The elephants would be too heavy and slow them down and destroy the footing for foot soldiers. Perhaps they can try wraith riders with their wyverns—should investigate further about the use of them. As he turned to head north to Skelbaka, he wrapped his turban over his face, guarding it from the cold winds.

Magnus did not sit idly since Snjofell left. He contacted the kingdom architect, Gormur, and commanded that plans needed to be established in the event of all-war. Gormur suggested that the dwarfs should commence on a new invention of his: iron boats. The boats would run on steam and be powered by coal, and as they would be constructed of iron, any wooden ships would

---

14 After the last Great Wars, the North Alliance and the southern kingdoms set up demilitarized zones.

easily fall prey by the new iron boats. Of course, he needed to construct them right away, not to mention that the coal ores needed to be mined. He showed the plans and ordered the plan be executed immediately.

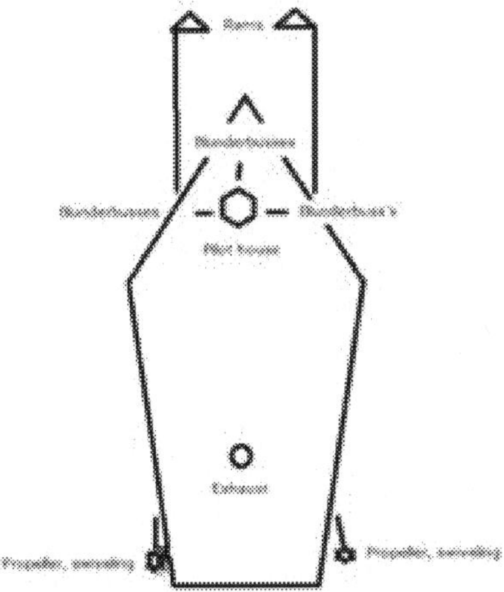

"We can ship them in pieces and put them together in Bátslipa," commented Magnus. "We can use them to ship supplies to Temple Uppsala too."

Baldur was standing next to the stables when one of the sentries on the wall shouted "Riders!" Baldur climbed the wall and observed two riders, one on a white mare and the other on a palomino. He smiled while he waited for Snjofell and Agnar to enter the fortress. "Greetings, my old friends," Baldur greeted them when they arrived. "I guess Biggy isn't with you. Did he quit or did he stay in Vokva?"

"Nay, we left him with the rest of the group in the castle. What news?" Snjofell had dismounted and was dusting off his robes. "We can sure use some refreshments."

Baldur recalled the events of the last week as he accompanied Snjofell and Agnar to Boars Head. "I will be leaving in the morrow, going to meet Lady Zonda. Apparently, the citadel is a wasp's nest of spies," added Baldur.

"Ah, as to be expected," Snjofell responded. "Svaramin knows that I have come to the defenses of the realm. We are going to meet with the Dark Elves."

The trio entered the Boars Head and immediately observed some gnomes and dwarfs cutting silk and weaving the silk into the armors. Espying Gagns, Baldur whistled to him, causing him to blink toward the trio.

"G-g-greetings," stammered Gagns. "Biggy isn't w-w-w-w-with you?"

Agnar replied, "No, he is with the rest of the group in Castle Vokva. We were snowed in for a few days. Got any meal and drink for us?"

"C-c-c-c-c-coming right up." And Gagns blinked into the kitchen.

Snjofell turned toward Baldur and said, "Take good care when you meet, you can trust no one. King Magnus shares your distrust of Queen Audri. At least he has gotten the warning and will increase the patrols around the castle."

After the refreshments, Gagns sat at the table and swapped tales of the previous week. "Did you ever meet SiSi?" Agnar asked of Gagns. "She was full of spunk, quite a handful for Biggy." He laughed.

"I met her one time p-p-previously, and I c-c-c-can't figure how he g-g-g-got hooked up with h-h-her," replied Gagns, half laughing. "I think h-h-he was half t-t-t-thinking he was trying t-t-to dump her."

"How are the Konglos?" Agnar asked Gagns as he downed a mug of mead. "Have you been out to the farm recently?"

"I p-p-put 'em in t-t-the corral here in t-t-the stables," Gagns absently replied. "I can c-c-control 'em anyway. Patrols g-go every day b-by there."

A few hours later, Snjofell and Agnar mounted their steeds and headed to the Coven.

Dabs and his group finally had a break from the snowfall. The four of them, riding their miniature ponies, left the safety of the castle walls. They had decided to first go to Fort Gate-Pass to spend the night in safety. They were passed by oxen-driven carts loaded with goods for selling in Vokva. The roads were much narrower as the mountains loomed about them, and the snow deepened since fewer inhabitants were using the road. The mountaintops were shrouded with clouds, and the temperatures were falling as they trekked up the paths.

Biggy, as a precaution, summoned his Sekhmet, Attafot. On a ledge above them, they could see wild mountain sheep frolicking. None of the group was talking as the cold winds had turned their beards and hair into whisps of ice. SiSi stayed next to Biggy on the journey, smiling occasionally when he met her gaze. The trip slowed terribly as the snow hampered their progress. Ahead, the fork in the road appeared with a sign pointing to the left, saying "Ferry Landing," and to the right, with a dilapidated sign indicating "Jarnsmiða Forge." Straight ahead was their destination, Fort Gate-Pass. After traveling several hundred meters, Dabs raised his right hand, indicating that something was ahead. He dismounted and studied the huge paw print in the snow, saying, "Looks like snow yeti . . . They always travel in packs. Smari, why don't you blink ahead, see if you can locate them." Smari dismounted and blinked ahead, possibly twenty meters ahead, and crouched.

Smari blinked back and announced, "Three of 'em. Looks like they killed a mountain sheep, and they are eating it. Just around of the bend, behind a boulder. They are vicious and huge."

"Hm . . . We can't go around 'em because of the mountain . . . And they will attack us on sight. SiSi, try and climb this big boulder, and I'll attack the nearest one . . . You should use the fear spell to disperse the group. Biggy, have your Sekhmet guard SiSi," instructed Dabs.

SiSi blinked to the peak of the boulder and signaled, "Let's do this."

Dabs sneaked down the path as he un-shouldered his blunderbuss. The snow yetis were covered with white fur; they had black eyes and two long fangs protruding from their lower jaws. Creeping within range, he gave out a bellowing roar as the three snow yetis charged. Dabs let out a volley from his weapon, wounding the lead snow yeti. The enraged beast continued at full speed toward Dabs. SiSi pulled her hands to her chest, and throwing her hands toward the charging beasts, she casted a fear spell. Two of the snow yetis stopped in their tracks as the beasts cowered in fear, turning tail and running away. Dabs unsheathed his sword, charged the remaining snow yeti, and smote a killing blow upon the animal.

The group reorganized. They took to work in skinning the beast, pulling its teeth and eyeballs. "Make some fur coats. If an alchemist shop is in the village, it will make some gold for us," commented Dabs. He knew that alchemists grind up the teeth and eyeballs in various potions. Finishing the skinning, the group returned to the path toward Fort Gate-Pass.

They entered the village outside of Fort Gate-Pass. It was seen as a small village. The military garrison was a small outpost rather than a fort and was rather dilapidated and run down with need of repairs. A few of troops of the realm seemed to be a scurvy lot, unkempt and sporting ill-kept armor and weapons. There was no hustle-and-bustle attitude like in Castle Vokva; there were no sounds of laughter or ambiance of warmth.

Finding the inn, named Dragonhead Inn, they entered and inquired about some shelter and food.

Dabs had talked with the owner, a fellow dwarf, and escorted the group to a table, where they ordered a meal. The inn was rather dreary with few decor but did offer warmth from the fireplace. Dabs excused himself from the table and walked to the bar. He engaged in conversation for a few minutes, returning with a scowl on his face. "Seems like that the fort is poorly managed and with low morale. Looks like desertions were high with the deserters hiding in the mountains. They are now bandits as they cannot reenter society for fear of arrest. Apparently, Queen Audri assigns troops here as punishment, and the realm poorly supports the fort," said Dabs. "I could only have one room, so it will be uncomfortable for the night, especially with Attafot in the room with us."

Soon after finishing the meal, they retired for the evening before commanding Attafot to guard duty.

Joldugrof was located in the farm belt around Castle Hearthglen. It was a fairly large farm, supporting cattle, pigs, and sheep. Baldur scouted the area before actually entering the farmlands, and having nothing aroused his suspicions, he dismounted his steed and walked to the barn. Zonda waved toward Baldur, and the two soon embraced and exchanged greetings. She was alone, and she had arranged for the owner of the farm to be out in the fields doing chores. "I have allies within the castle, but any move will result in bloodshed. I fear that the realm's defenses have been compromised and, from rumors within the castle walls, indicate that the elves will not fight. The dwarfs are leery towards the kingdom, and other than commerce, the gnomes have little reason to come to our aid," Zonda sadly stated. The two had neared the barn doors, and she added, "What should we do?"

"Zonda, I really—" Baldur started to say, but the barn doors flew open and royal troops swarmed them. Baldur threw his sword-hand toward the hilt of his sword but stopped as twenty soldiers brandished their weapons. Baldur exchanged questioning eyes with Zonda but said nothing.

The squad leader came forth and stated, "You two are under arrest for treason to the throne! Disarm immediately." And he motioned the soldiers to bind both Baldur and Zonda. Baldur opened his mouth to speak, but he was clubbed on his head, silencing him. Zonda was dragged to a mount and was told to keep silent on the ride to the citadel. Baldur was slung over a mount, and the captives were led away.

He stood before Ormskepna and Queen Audri, his hands still bound behind him. To the right was Zonda, but not bound. Queen Audri rose and pointed toward Zonda. She yelled, "Zonda, my most trusted lady-in-waiting! How have you come to this? You to consort with and conspiring with traitors! Have I not treated you well?" The queen had a scorn on her face.

"I Have not conspired with traitors, I only wanted to help the realm," responded Zonda.

"You WANTED to help the realm . . . Why? Am I not the queen of the realm? Do you think YOU can make decisions on your own? What should be your punishment? Is it death or imprisonment?" The queen was emanating blind fury toward Zonda.

Ormskepna bent over and whispered in her ear as she nodded before voicing her decision. The queen seemed to have lost some of her rage and said, "My decision, as queen of the realm, deems you guilty, and you will be placed under house arrest." She signaled to the sentries, and Zonda was escorted out of the throne room. "And you, you disgusting worm of a man, what say you?"

"Your Highness, I feared for the realm as we are on verge of open war. I will not apologize for my actions!" Baldur stated with a firm voice. "Do with me as you wish." The haughtiness in his voice enflamed Ormskepna, and for a second, his scorn for Baldur was apparent.

Ormskepna relaxed his facial features and whispered to the queen. She nodded in agreement, and she whispered back. "Traitor Baldur, my decision by royal decree is that you be demoted to a foot soldier, and that you shall be incarcerated for your crimes, to spend your lifetime in the dungeon." The queen beckoned to the soldiers to have them escort Baldur to the dungeon. "Be glad that I have shown you some mercy."

Agnar, Snjofell, and Afmyndur met with Bogamaður in a clearing in Sko Forest. The Sko Forest had a light dusting of snow on the ground, with the treetops glistening because of it. Bogamaður was a few years older than Agnar, with olive-hued skin, brown hair. Bogamaður knew Snjofell from encounters when he was younger, and he was pleased as he knew that he could be trusted. Agnar, because he was half human, was not trusted, and the major topics of the discussions were excluding Agnar. Snjofell entrusted Bogamaður with the developments of the last weeks, and the subject of relinquishing the hilt was hitting a snag. Apparently, the Dark Elves will not be open to allowing nonelven participations.

"If you will not agree to lose the hilt, then how about you bringing the hilt in person? I would agree to not touching the sword," suggested Agnar to Bogamaður.

"That is a step in the right direction, but if the Dark Elves disagree, then we are still in an impasse." Pausing a second, Bogamaður added, "What if you bring the sword to me? I can attach the hilt, thus, we can grant unification as long as no human touches it. It will be a hard sell, but I think I can get the rest of them to agree to that . . . But after the Gjaldi swindled our race, humans can never be involved. Even at that, I doubt that the elves support any military action in defense of the human realm."

"I may be half human, but my allegiance is to the elves. I will swear an oath to the king of the elves that I will never take sides with the humans over the elves. I grew up in the elves clans, but I was a product of human and elven. I owe nothing to the human side," swore Agnar.

Agnar seemed to be at ease with the statements and asked Snjofell to speak to him private. After returning after the consultation, Bogamaður turned to Agnar and said, "It seems that you will be true to your word. I will wait for your fire signals, and you can turn the sword over to me on the meeting spot here in Sko Forest. Hopefully, I can convince the other Dark Elves to stop the division amounts the clans."

Dabs and his company left Fort Gate-Pass toward Jarnsmiða. The winds and snow had let up, making travel much easier. In the distance, the Forge seemed to be swallowed in a perpetual fog, with occasional breaks that allowed the shape of the Forge to be seen. The mountains on the left were impassable, at least not with the mounts. Occasionally, the group could see the light from the sun reflecting on the snow-peak pinnacles. Their mounts were laboring, with puffs of steam through their nostrils; other than that, they were making good progress. Dabs reigned in his mount, waiting for the rest of the group to near. Whispering to the troop, Dabs said, "We are being followed . . . up to the left. Ready your weapons in case there is trouble. It looks like we have met some of the bandits." The four members proceeded at a slow pace.

Two humans appeared just ahead, standing in the path. "Whoa," stated Dabs to his mount. "If you intend harm, we are well armed!" yelled Dabs toward the two people blocking the path. "Tell us what you want."

The leader of the humans shrugged and instructed, "Pay the toll, either gold or Ten-Sheckles, and I will allow you to pass." The two were rather scraggly-looking, thin and hungry-looking, with long unkempt beards and hair. Their worn clothing was in need of repair.

"I'll pay you nothing!" roared Dabs. "I will sheathe our weapons if you do the same. I will give you food for exchange of information."

Peering through squinted eyes, he said with distrust, "And if I decide to run you through and just take your possessions?"

Dabs considered it for a moment as the two were weak, poorly armed, and licking their lips. They were obviously bluffing, and Dabs stated, "I wish you no harm! But if you want a fight, we will make quick work of you. Stand down, and I will feed you. I only need information about Jarnsmiða Forge."

The leader of the humans whispered to the other and, after a few moments, said, "I will sheathe my weapons then. Throw the food to me, and I will answer your questions." He reconsidered attacking, glancing toward Attafot, plus the blunderbuss, and fearing the sword Dabs had.

Dabs reached into his rucksack and threw several loafs of flaxen bread and several sticks of jerky. The humans devoured the food as the troop dismounted and neared the two bandits. "What lies ahead?" Dabs asked.

They responded between mouthfuls. "Dreadful place, nothing but death—horrible death. Even if you can make it past the carnivorous vines, you will face the skeleton warriors, not to mention the vampire bats," explained the bandit with wide eyes and fear. "No manner of living person has returned. The stench of death awaits you. Then you will meet your match when you meet the Shiva. I advise you to turn back while you can still do so."

"Nay, we shall not return back . . . just a moment," replied Dabs as he retrieved the snow-yeti fur. "Here, take this. It will at least you warm."

The leader of the bandits grinned from ear to ear as he caught the fur pelt in midair. "Thank you, Sire, and if you ever need any help, if I can, I will return the favor," the human said.

"There will be two riders coming this way within the next days, one on a white mare and the other on a palomino, do not delay them," instructed Dabs. Thanking the bandits for their information, the troop mounted their steeds and proceeded toward Jarnsmiða.

After riding for three hours, Dabs found a clearing ahead and decided to camp for the night. The vegetation was sparse there, with the exception for patches of lichens and moss. After a meager meal, the company bedded down, waiting for Snjofell and Agnar.

VII

Jarnsmiða is formidable, thought Agnar to himself as he used his looking glass to survey the ruins. The outer walls were decayed and had fallen in several places, showing boulders and strange, eerie rock formations. There were no discernible life forms around the Forge except for thick brownish vines swallowing the stone buildings. They looked like thin gnarled fingers as they tried to grasp the erected walls, as if to squeeze the life from the constructions. There were no birds nesting or flying about; there were no animals chattering about, like the silent emptiness of death. The dense fog surrounding the Forge seemed to envelop from the peaks of the mountains down toward the ground.

Agnar let out a slight whistle and announced to the group, "Wow, this place is a total wreck. It seems to me that nothing is stirring out there, kind of a dead place." Agnar handed the looking glass to Snjofell. "Take a look at the ledge just over the courtyard."

Snjofell gazed through the looking glass and said, Hm . . . Seems like ancient runes. I haven't been here for over a hundred years, so it is strange to me, at least not as I remember it was."

Dabs suggested that the group have a meal before taking the path leading to the courtyard. "There are carnivorous vines about, so we should go on foot from now on."

After the meal was finished, the group unpacked their mounts and tethered them in the clearing. Biggy commanded "Heim" to his Sekhmet since the vines would target him.

The troop drudged forward toward the Forge, armed with swords unsheathed. Shortly after progressing several a hundred yards, the vines appeared, like slithering snakes on the path. Just off the path were several pods, which had arm-like vines attached. The arms writhed as they sensed along on the path, seeking innocent prey. Around the pods were remnants of bodies: an arm bone here and there, some leg bones, some skulls with jaws open, as if they were screaming in their death throes. Some of them had portions of armor, a few weapons and shields, all decayed with rust.

Biggy uttered, "What a way to die." They commenced hacking and cutting at the vines as they needed to clear the path. Dabs voiced a warning to the group, "Keep an eye out for the vines. If they grab you, you'll be sucked into the pods." For almost two hours, they hacked away until the outer walls appeared before them. The wall was constructed of stone blocks and mortar, approximately twenty feet in height. The wall was so weak that any slight touch sent blocks falling from the bulwark. The dank air swirled about them and seemed to whisper "Go away" to the company. The only sounds in the area were the slight breezes with the occasional plop of crumbling construction materials falling. The group was on edge, ever alert for danger.

Snjofell said in a low voice, "If I recall correctly, the main gate should be over here to the right. Through there, we should be in the courtyard. Keep your guard up. Biggy, blink up onto the wall, see what you find . . . and be careful of your footing."

Upon striding the wall, he held up seven fingers, pointing off to the right, and again, straight ahead. "Seven skeleton warriors, one skeleton fire mage," he whispered.

As Biggy turned to blink down, a block crumbled from the wall. He yelled "Haaallllllp!" And he fell with a thud, falling into a slump. SiSi immediately cried "Biggyyyy!" and instantly blinked to the wall and jumped down to assist Biggy. Agnar commanded Bangsi "Komdu" as he scampered to the gate entrance. Dabs unsheathed his sword, running simultaneously behind Agnar. Bangsi, with his razor-sharp teeth and claws, was already making quick work on the rotten wooden gate.

As the aggressors turned to attack, Biggy commanded "Komdu," and freed Attafot while SiSi summoned a freeze spell, freezing the fire mage in his tracks. The skeletons—some with sword and shield, others with bows—came in attack mode with ferocity.

The bones clattered while their jaws uttered an empty clatter, as if the teeth were gnawing, weapons drawn. Attafot engaged two of them, gluing them to the ground as Bangsi leaped on their backs, which resulted in a sickening sound of bones crashing to the ground. SiSi grabbed Biggy roughly, threw him over her shoulder, and ran toward the gate entrance. Dabs charged two of the skeleton warriors, roaring mightily, leaping through the air, twisting in flight as the two were hewn in two. The remaining two skeletons were targeted by Agnar, who loosened dual arrows. *Thwump-thwump* sang the missiles directly into their skulls. Dabs attacked the frozen fire mage with a volley of his broadsword, killing it instantly.

Biggy cried in pain as he grasped his right leg. "Broken . . . It's broken."

Dabs rushed to assist Biggy, bending down to confirm the diagnosis. "This will hurt," warned Biggy and set the bone. Biggy wailed a cry of pain as SiSi tried to comfort him. "Don't move," Biggy heard Dabs' instructions. He then used his paladin lay-on-hands technique. Biggy instantly felt the pain lessen. Dabs then applied a mage bandage to the leg and said, "You will be fine in about ten minutes."

Snjofell then indicated that the two Sekhmet should remain with the party as danger had not lessened. He reconnoitered the courtyard, having seen nothing except for debris from the buildings and stone statues. Many of the statues, once proud stone icons of dwarven heroes, were dilapidated; some whole while others were just half statues. The air was stolid, eerily so, with guard shacks and roofs that had collapsed. Ahead was the entrance into the Forge. The dwarfs had constructed their dwellings inside of the cave as they chose to live underground. The Forge had been constructed by chiseling the city directly into the face of the mountain.

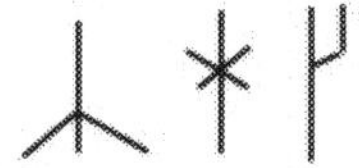

Snjofell then read the runes they had seen earlier. "Þór hammer forge," translated Snjofell. "That is the inscription you had seen earlier. Over here." He pointed toward a massive stone door hewed into the mountain. There were skeleton remains scattered throughout the courtyard. There were human skeletons, orc bones, and numerous dwarfs partially clad in various armors and weapons. "Perhaps scavengers or archeologists, maybe bandits," added Snjofell.

Biggy was feeling better as he had healed enough to test it by putting weight upon it. "I sure am glad that you came along. The fire mage would have done me in for sure. One blast with a fireball would have surely killed me," he said to SiSi. His leg was sore, and he still hobbled slightly, but he wasn't worse for better. She grinned as she looked at Biggy.

Dabs smiled and stood up, saying, "Smari, why don't you blink out there near the door. And be careful, lots of dangerous things around still and falling debris. Agnar, yield me your looking glass." He scanned the area around the great door, paying attention to the carved open slots used by sentries. "Bats," he said as he swung to the left toward the mountaintops. "Wyverns, coming this way!" shouted Dabs as he grabbed Biggy and herded the group out toward an abandoned guard shack. Smari had already blinked to safety. After the company of heroes dove under cover in the building, they observed wraith riders mounted on wyverns. "Don't move lest they catch your movements," whispered Dabs.

The wyverns circled around the courtyard, examining the newly found skeleton warriors. The constant shrieks from them were annoying while Agnar and Biggy were comforting their Sekhmets lest they attack. The stench from their wings was overpowering when one of them flew near. "Three of 'em," whispered Snjofell as one of them landed and dismounted. He was about the size of a human, cloaked in black cottony material, and with armor-plated tipped boots and armor-plated gloves. Their facial features were nonexistent, as if the hood was but a ghostly head. The other two wraith riders were circling about, constantly on the lookout for movements. Eventually, the three rejoined above the great door, satisfied that nothing was to be found. They returned to the north.

"That was close," said Dabs to the group. They assembled and headed out for the door. As the troop neared the door, Snjofell issued a warning. In front of them was Stone Shiva,[15] looking like a lion with four arms but with a human head. "Don't move," Snjofell admonished the group. "The Shiva will kill all of us unless you let me do the talking." Already, the Shiva was aroused, looking toward the company. "Don't scatter, keep together." Snjofell walked toward the Shiva as it hissed, "I see you are back, Snjofell, or whatever you are called now."

15 Shiva was an ancient statue that would riddle passersby, and if the wrong answer was given, the Shiva would kill them.

VIII

Dungeons are disgusting, thought Baldur. He had been there for about five days, a week maybe, and the stench from sweat, feces, and urine was nauseating. The dungeon was constructed belowground with iron bars covering the air vents above. The cells were covered in hay, which was used for both bedding and comfort from the cold. The poor lighting, mostly from wall-embedded torches, gave a dark, forbidding texture to it. The dungeon held about fifty-five prisoners, with him being in the only single-occupancy cell, probably because of his rank at the time of his arrest. The furnishings consist of a pail, to relieve him, and a metal bowl/plate and cup to drink from. The prisoners were fed once a day, and once a week, they were sent single file out into the prisoner yard for a washing.[16] Rarely were prisoners afforded visits, but those affluent individuals could gain access by bribes. From the first day of his incarceration, he set up an exercise program as a means of keeping his physical and mental health up to par.

---

16 Washing consisted of being hosed down to control lice and disease.

The other prisoners knew that he was a special guest, and they greeted him with scowls and profane, provoking language. Eventually, they came to accept the fact that he was a prisoner and not a spy. The closest prisoner to his cell, named Stephan, recounted his misdeeds. In fact, most of them, as Stephan told him, were political prisoners. Almost all of them in there had displeased the regime, and very few actually committed acts of a criminal nature. Stephan said that fifty-three of them were human and two were dwarfs. The regime did not want to deal with the various races, and they were executed or sent to their own kingdoms. One exception was for mages; they were executed immediately as they could not control the spell casting from them. The hunters were kept in special cells with ward stones,[17] which blocked their telepathic abilities so they couldn't summon their sekhmet. Stephan related that he was stationed in Fort Gate-Pass and that he tried to desert his post but was captured. He retold that hundreds of soldiers had deserted and that the post was cursed. The commander of the post was a drunken sod, and he did nothing for the troops under his command.

"I vow toward every single one of you that if I ever leave here alive, you are coming with me!" Baldur swore an oath to Stephan that he would not abandon them.

---

17 Ward stones are magically embedded spells that break spells or prevent actions, depending upon the spell. For example, a ward stone can prevent gnomes to blink or a hunter to summon his Sekhmet.

"I have heard those empty promises before," retorted Stephan. "How are you intending to get out? Escape is impossible from this rat hole."

Zonda was miserable as she had been betrayed by the queen and Ormskepna. She had all the comforts of home, but she was prohibited neither to allow visitors nor to leave her quarters. She was depressed and wondered how she could escape, especially from that cur Ormskepna, as he offered her freedom but at a price. She rebuffed him and threw him out of her quarters. The very thought of him touching her shot bolts of revulsion through her. She thought of Agnar, imagining the horrors he was experiencing. In her mind's eye, she pictured when she first met him: an honorable and decent man. She could at least explain their impediment; she then scurried to her desk and took pen to paper.

Baldur

I am writing you to let you know that I had nothing to do with arrest of ourselves. I was just as shock as you were. I trust that you are as well as can be expected. I am truly sorry that the events overtook us, and I did not betray you. I only wish that we had met under different circumstances; I found you honorable, of good stature, and I enjoyed in your presence. If we ever meet again, please do not think unkindly of me.

Sincerely,

Zonda

She then sealed the message and called for one of her aides. When her aide had the message, she gave twenty ten-sheckles to the aide and said, "This is for the dungeon guard. Deliver this to Baldur."

Svaramin received the scouting report from Salim-Dug. While he was reading the report, an orc sentry entered the room and signaled that he wished to speak to Salim-Dug. The sentry conversed for a moment and waved him off, and Salim-Dug returned. "Sire, I received a message that some of our spies reported a small band of mixed race had recently contact with bandits near Jarnsmiða Forge. Apparently, there was a human, a dwarf, and four gnomes, which were asking about the Forge," said Salim-Dug. "The human was riding a palomino steed, and the others, miniature ponies."

"Hmm . . . A dwarf, a human, and some gnomes . . . interesting," said Svaramin. "And what were they asking about?"

Salim-Dug shrugged his shoulders and said, "Nothing special, just how do they get there. Probably just some plunderers or archaeologists."

"Send out some wraith riders, scout around the Forge. You are probably correct, just someone looking for loot . . . But if they aren't, try to find out what they are up to. We know that Snjofell was in Castle Vokva," said Svaramin in an interrogative tone.

The black tower had another floor added to it, one with a balcony. After finishing reading the report,

Svaramin advised, "Wonderful, wonderful . . . I always thought I could depend upon you. The advice you offered about the elephants is excellent. Too bad that the goblins will be of no use to us, they are stupid and don't have the attention span to make good soldiers. We should make some plans before open war commences." He walked onto the balcony and peered over the landscape and thought, "How about assault by sea?"

IX

Shiva spoke with a detached and cold voice to Snjofell. "Yes, I am back. And you haven't changed a bit," Snjofell sarcastically retorted. "What are you doing here? If I remember correctly, you were on a glacier near Jokla City."

"Oh, I roam at will . . . Did you ever find that ring you were looking for? Too bad I disintegrated two of your party." Shiva coughed as she spoke. "I warned you not to encircle me."

"Yes, and a warning I won't forget about. We are here to enter the Forge. I hope you have a harder riddle for me?" Snjofell knew that the Shiva would pose a riddle, and the wrong answer meant instant death to the entire troop.

As her eyes deepened to a red color, she asked, "I can be quick and then I'm deadly. I am a rock, shell, and bone medley. If I were made into a man, I'd make people dream. I gather in my millions by ocean, sea, and stream. What am I?"

Snjofell lifted up his right hand as to silence any responses from the group. Quickly, she said, "Your answer?"

Snjofell responded, "Hoh, can you not do better? It is sand, of course."

Suddenly, the Shiva returned to a stone statue as the door creaked open. Beyond the door lay darkness, inviting unwary creatures to gain access to the treasures within. Of course, Snjofell had been inside on numerous occasions, but that was before they rendered the city uninhabitable. He would have to research his memories to find the route to the actual Forge. "In with you," commanded Snjofell as the group entered single file into the city.

As the commandos entered the city proper, the door slammed shut behind them. They were engulfed in total darkness as they knocked about the debris, which were remnants from the quakes. Snjofell tapped his cane on the floor, and suddenly, a pale ghostly light emanated from the cane's tip. The cavernous city entrance reverberated with echoes with each movement of the group. "I don't remember such emptiness," said Snjofell as they surveyed around them. The dust lay thick on the floor, with pieces of stone furniture strewn about. Even the thick spider webs were in every place. The cold dark air was thick and devoid of any sounds except for the intruders.

This area was obviously an entrance to a great city. Along the walls were stone statues, as if replicating their long-gone heroes. Numerous of them were toppled, as if they had been beheaded in mortal combat. As the group progressed along, there were faint tracks in the dust from the little creatures that now call this home. Each step threw dust into the air, making breathing difficult. To the left were fragments clinging from the ceiling, nothing but tattered rags from once-majestic banners.

"To the right used to be a meeting room, and dignitaries were greeted there. I suggest you to get rid of your Sekhmets . . . Don't want them to cause a cave in. Everything is so dilapidated and fragile. It would behoove us to not touch anything. Especially any stair casings will be suspect. Here, grab some torches from the walls, we will need them." Both Agnar and Biggy complied with his request.

The torches were lit, and the dancing flames casted eerie shadows around them. With life-giving light now affording much more effervescent light, it allowed the party to explore more area. They had found that, in places, the floor had buckled from the tremors, and they used caution when entering the rooms. Occasionally, they encountered vampire bats, though they were prevented from invading the group's space because of the torches. The stench from the bat guava was overpowering, and the place was swarming with scorpions, snakes, and worms.

"Ah, to the throne room," whispered Snjofell. Ahead, the wooden door was askew, half-fallen, as if it were trying to reach the safety of the doorframe. Dabs swept away the huge spider webs from the door with his sword. Inside, Dabs, with wide-eyed astonishment, said "By the gods" as he knelt on one knee and prayed next to the tomb of King Hauster. "Our ancestors," said Dabs, his throat swelling with emotion. He knelt for a few minutes while he examined the stone sarcophagus; the lid was heavily damaged from debris from the ceiling. He blew away the thick dust and then opened the coffin; he was awestruck! He cried out, "The Great Horn of Þór! Once again, the Great Horn will sound again in the house of the dwarfs!" He retrieved the horn, allocating some space within his rucksack.

As Dabs turned to return to the group, the ground shook, slightly, with the echoes of falling debris reverberating. Biggy stared at Snjofell and said, "Wow, maybe Eldfjall is warning us to go no farther."

Snjofell advised them to move along. "Yes, we need to get to our destination. The prophecies foretell of another eruption, and that the world will be dark once again. Come, the entrance to the Forge is not far now."

Following the hallway, cautiously, they trudged along. The pitch-black darkness was only sliced by the torches they carried. The group felt the loneliness of a hiker who had been lost, and with the dancing shadows from the torches, it enhanced the feeling. At last here they arrived at, the entrance to the Forge. Whispering under his breath, Dabs said, "Phew, I be glad when we can get out of here." He ran his hand across the walls to the entrance—and withdrew it quickly. "Yuck," he said, and then telling the group, "slime, and the smell, it's horrible."

Entering the Forge lobby, they found themselves looking down into a huge cavernous pit. Across the abyss was the Forge entrance. Scanning the room, Smari gave a cry, "Drawbridge! The lever is up here." Snjofell came to where Smari was standing and pulled down the lever. The clank of chains was apparent as the links cried out, reverberating throughout the room. There were three different doors that gained access to different areas of the Forge. A few moments later, the drawbridge thumped as it came to a rest across the chasm. "I suspect it isn't safe . . . Test each step," said Snjofell.

About halfway across the drawbridge, the group of adventurers was stopped in their tracks. Behind them, with no warning, was a snarling, roaring, one-eyed creature known as Oneauga.[18] It was twice as tall as a human, had an enraged single eye in the center of its head and a single sharp horn, and was bearing a double-bladed ax. It was wearing chain-link mail trousers, and each step it took made a sickly crunch. The barrel-sized arms were huge.

SiSi turn toward the Oneauga and threw a freeze spell. It slowed it down but did no noticeable damage to it. The Oneauga swung the ax as it charged

18 Oneauga is a Cyclops creature that devours people.

forward. Snjofell leveled his staff, and a bolt of lightning flew toward the Oneauga, but nothing—it was unstoppable. With each step, the drawbridge swayed, dangerously so. Snjofell spun toward the group and said, "**Fools, run, you fools!**" Then he spun back and leaped toward the monster, poising his cane. He struck the creature with his staff; the Oneauga lost its balance. The force from the striking staff and the weight from Snjofell resulted in the casting of the monster, and Snjofell fell into the chasm! Planks from the drawbridge fell as the duo dueled, and they flailed as they fell. The sickening screams of agony echoed from the abyss, into the throes of death itself. With flailing arms, the Oneauga could only gasp air. "Argggggggh!" as it dropped. The survivors were thrown in the air and, attempting to ride the wild animal of a drawbridge, ran as fast as they could, casting themselves forward toward the door, just as the creaking and swaying and groaning drawbridge snapped. Cries of "**Snjofell**" arose from the members as they watched helplessly as the two combatants fell into the black pit and were swallowed into the abyss.

Shocked, the survivors laid on the ground, catching their breaths. They could hardly believe their own eyes; their guide and mentor was gone. Dabs quickly took command, as he showed a true leader attribute, and assessed the situation. "Let's keep towards the forge. Snjofell will not be forgotten," he choked out the words. "Is everyone all right? Did anyone lose anything into the pit?" Everyone checked their possessions and tried to find if anyone was injured. The group declared that everything was intact and that there were no injuries.

Trying to get a glimpse of the disappearing Snjofell, SiSi wiped a tear from her eyes and said, "Bless ye, we will never forget you."

Agnar was wounded to his soul and came to attention and saluted toward the location Snjofell was last seen. "Aye, let us leave this accursed place. But to where? More importantly, how do we get back?"

No one had an answer.

The world had come full circle. The banging of the drumbeat of war was upon them. The winds of change would be upon them forever, with the accompaniment of the dark, evil wind. The alliances of the south had shattered, with the inhabitants looking toward leadership that was no more. Long-sought peace was no more, being replaced with belligerence, distrust, and open conflict. Such is the price of evil versus good. With the loss of peace, the world had forgotten the price of war; the price of peace is eternal vigilance.

GLOSSARY

Dobamen. Race of humanoids with dark skin and warts and are cannibalistic in nature.

Ápstil. Race of humanoids dark brown in color and known for its riding steeds. Ruthless and cunning, they are Bedouin in nature.

Attafot. Biggys giant konglo

Aura: Monetary amount (one hundred aura equals ten-Sheckles)

Bangsi. Agnar's wolverine Sekhmet

Blafjall Mountains: Located just south of Fort Hermana

Bleusgrof. Farm owned by Biggy

Closu. Agnar's horse

Dabbilus. Dwarven Paladin, called Dabs for short.

Dragonhead Inn. Inn in the Fort Gate-Pass village

Dwarfs. Stunted humanoid with extraordinary strength. Generally, they live underground and create magnificent things using a hammer and chisel. They mine ores and gems from the ground, use forges, and are excellent armor producers.

Elves. Pale-skinned Race of inhabitants that are pale with pointy ears. They are attuned to nature itself.

Foringi. Second in command at Ft. Hermana

Flugarpets. Flying mounts

Gemshard Heart: Precious gems that are used to bolster armor.

Gnomes: Knee-high (to humans) race that uses science to invent. They are good in accounting as well as banking.

Goblins. Race of creatures (similar to dwarfs in size) that is excellent in working with the sciences. They are dark-green skinned with pointy ears and have no hair.

Gufaheita. Steam-generated hot pits around geothermal areas

Hestur. Mounts (can be horses, donkeys, cattle, or eagles, in the case of good characters; can be fiery steeds, mountain goats, water buffalo, bats, or rocs, in the case of evil).

Heitapipur. Steam pipes used by dwarfs in their forges.

Humans. Race of people that are generally tall and have good military and organizational skills.

Hauster. King of Jarnsmiða

Jarnsmiða Forge. Dwarven iron forge factory

Jokla City. North Alliance city inhabited by Orcs and trolls and ogres

Joldugrof. Farm located north of Egilsstað

Konglo. Spiders, giant web-weaving creatures

Komdu. Order given for the Sekhmet to appear

Mage bandages. Used by healers and constructed by bolts of mage cloth

Mjolnir. The Great Sword forged by the dwarfs

Ogres. Race with huge, muscular heavy-set bodies, with two fangs protruding from their lower jaw. They are rather slow intellectually and hard to antagonize.

Oneauga. Cyclops in the Forge

Orcs. Race that is aggressive and militarized. They have greenish-hued skin, generally with two fangs protruding from their lower jaw. Almost always with a crop of black hair braided on the head.

Ormskepna. Evil adviser

Rikard. Prisoner who befriended Baldur

Salim-Dug. Ápstil commander

Sekhmet: Pet (can be cats, dogs, wolverines, bats, or apes). scandium. The great ore given by Thor for forging the Great Sword, Mjolnir

Shiva. Sphinx of Jarnsmiða

SiSi. Biggy's girlfriend

Skelbaka. Outpost for the North Alliance

Sko Forest. Elven forest where they live

Smakongur. King of the gnomish people and the Kingdom Jotheim

Stephan. Prisoner who befriended Baldur

Svartaturn. The new black tower used by Svaramin

Ten-Sheckles. Monetary amount used

Two-Fishes Inn. Tavern in Castle Vokva

Trolls. Race of inhabitants similar to Ogres, usually used in manual labor.